JACK
~ and the ~
BEANSTALK
◆ Alan Garner ◆
Illustrated by Julek Heller

A Doubleday Book for Young Readers

For Robert

A Doubleday Book for Young Readers

Published by
Delacorte Press
Bantam Doubleday Dell Publishing Group, Inc.
666 Fifth Avenue
New York, New York 10103

Doubleday and the portayal of an anchor with a dolphin
are trademarks of Bantam Doubleday Dell Publishing Group, Inc.

This work was first published in Great Britain in 1992 by
HarperCollins Publishers Ltd

Text copyright © 1992 by Alan Garner
Illustrations copyright © 1992 by Julek Heller

Library of Congress Cataloging in Publication Data

Garner, Alan [date of birth]
Jack and the Beanstalk / Alan Garner ; illustrated by Julek Heller.
p.   cm.
Summary: A boy climbs to the top of a giant beanstalk,
where he uses his quick wits to outsmart an ogre and make
his and his mother's fortune.
ISBN0-385-30693-8
[1. Fairy tales.   2. Folklore–England.   3. Giants–Folklore.]
I. Heller, Julek, ill.   II. Title
PZ8. G226Jac 1992
398.2–dc20
[E]   91-36717 CIP AC
Manufactured in Great Britain
October 1992
13579108642
HCL

Once upon a time Jack and his mother lived on a common in a poor tumbledown house of sorts, with only a white cow to keep them. Every day Jack picked up snapping wood and sticks for the fire; his mother dug the garden; and the white cow grazed the lane side.

But one morning Jack's mother said, "Jack," she said, "the crock's empty; the garden's bare; we've got no meat; we've got no money; and the white cow is dry. You must take her to the market and sell her."

So off went Jack with the white cow to market, but he had not gone far when he met a man on the road.

"Where are you going, Jack?" said the man.

"I'm going to market," said Jack, "to sell the white cow."

"Well," said the man, "I'll give you more than you'll get at the market. If you'll sell me your white cow, I'll give you five beans – that's what I'll give you."

"Well," said Jack, "for five beans, you may have the white cow. Mother will be pleased!"

The man took five beans from his hat and gave them to Jack; and Jack gave the man the white cow and went back home.

When Jack's mother saw him coming, she said, "You're soon back. You've never been to market. Where's our white cow?"

"I met a man on the road," said Jack, "and he bought her."

"How much did he give you?" said Jack's mother.

"He gave me five beans," said Jack.

"What?" said Jack's mother. "He gave you five beans for that white cow?"

"He did," said Jack.

"You great gobbin fool!" said Jack's mother. "Now we can all starve!"

And she took the beans and threw them out of the window, and they both went to bed without supper that night.

In the morning when Jack woke up, the house was as black as a bag. He lay on his bed and waited for the sun to come. He waited and he waited; the cocks were crowing, but the sun never came. He waited some more; and still it didn't come. Jack got off his bed and opened the door.

The sun was high and shining, and it made Jack blink. He blinked again when he saw what was up.

The house was covered over by a great beanstalk. It turned about the door-hole and over the window, the walls, the roof, and round the smokestack into the sky; and however much he leaned and peered and scanned his eyes, Jack couldn't see the top of the beanstalk. It shoved among the clouds and went beyond.

"Well," said Jack, "Mother will be pleased!" And he started to climb the beanstalk.

Jack climbed, and he climbed, and he climbed; he climbed up, and up, and up, and up; up, up, up Jack went.

He went past weathercocks and larks, higher than the swallows he went, up, up in the air, till at last he came to the top of the beanstalk and the end of the sky.

There was a land at the top of the beanstalk: rocks and trees and hills; and a road stretched across the land to a castle far away on a cliff. Jack set off along the road, and by the time he reached the castle he was wearied. He knocked at the castle door, and a big woman opened it.

"What do you want?" said the big woman.

"Meat and drink," said Jack.

"You can't come in here," said the big woman. "My man's a giant, and he eats people. He'll be home presently."

"No matter of that," said Jack. "I'm famished."

So the big woman let Jack into the castle and fed him bread and cheese and small beer. But he'd scarcely finished that when he heard a hubbub and to-do outside: bump! bump! bump! it went.

"What's all the commotion?" said Jack.

"That's my man," said the big woman. "You'd best hide in the oven, and quickly."

Jack went and hid in the oven. No sooner done than the giant came in, and a great hairy giant he was too, and he sniffed, and he said:

"Fee! Fi! Fo! Fum!
I smell the blood of an Englishman!
Be he alive, or be he dead,
I'll grind his bones to make my bread!"

"Nothing of the sort," said the big woman. "It's your breakfast in the bailey. You sit yourself down while I fetch it."

The big woman went off to the bailey
for the giant's breakfast, and the giant
sat at the table and he said, "I smell fresh
meat." But the big woman came back with
his breakfast, and he ate it all up, first and
last. And when he had finished, he said to
the big woman, "Time I was counting my
gold."

"You sit still," said the big woman.
"I'll get it."

She opened a trunk, and brought the giant his gold, tied up in two sacks; and the giant tipped it onto the table and counted it all. Then, when the giant had counted his gold and put it back in the sacks, he laid his head on the table and went to sleep.

Out from the oven popped Jack. He picked up the two sacks of gold, put one under his arm and the other on his shoulder, and off he ran, out of the castle, along the road, across the land, and all the way back to the beanstalk. He climbed down the beanstalk, down, down, right into his mother's garden, and went to show her what he'd got.

Now Jack and his mother had the giant's gold, and were living well. But sooner or later the day came when Jack thought he would climb the beanstalk again; so up the beanstalk he marched, went straight to the giant's castle, and knocked at the door. The big woman opened it; and she looked at Jack and she said, "Who are you?"

"One who's famished," said Jack.

"Wasn't it you I fed before?" said the big woman. "And didn't you run off with my man's gold?"

"No, I never," said Jack; and he went in and sat himself down, while the big woman fetched him a helping of cold ham and a jug of buttermilk. Jack polished off the lot. But before he could ask for more, he heard another hubbub and to-do outside: bump! bump! bump! And the big woman said, "That's my man. You'd best hide in the oven, and quickly."

Jack went and hid in the oven. The great hairy giant came in and sniffed, and he said:

"Fee! Fi! Fo! Fum!
I smell the blood of an Englishman!
Be he alive, or be he dead,
I'll grind his bones to make my bread!"

"Nothing of the sort," said the big woman. "It's your dinner in the dungeon."

"I smell fresh meat," said the giant. And he roamed about the kitchen, sniffing, but he never found Jack in the oven.

The big woman brought the giant his dinner, and he ate it up, first and last; then he said, "I want my hen."

The big woman said, "You sit still. I'll get it." She went to the corner and came back with a red hen in her hands, and she put it on the table.

The giant said to the red hen, "Lay."
And the hen went and laid an egg of
gold on the table. "Lay," said the giant.
And the hen laid another golden egg.

"Lay," said the giant; and she did it again.
"That'll do," said the giant, and he put his
head down on his arms, and soon he was
snoring fit to shake the castle.

Jack nipped out of the oven, put the hen under his arm, the gold eggs in his pocket, and ran. He ran all the way till he came to the top of the beanstalk. Down he went, into his mother's garden, to show her what he'd got.

So there they were, the pair of them, with the red hen laying gold eggs, and everything cozy. But the day came when Jack thought he must have another go on the beanstalk. He left his mother behind, and up he marched again to the land at the top, and along the road to the castle. This time, though, he didn't knock at the door; he waited outside. And presently the big woman came to fetch the washing in off the line; and while she was doing that, Jack sneaked into the kitchen and hid in the copper.

The big woman came back and hung the washing on the maiden by the fire, and began to get the giant's tea. Then it wasn't long before bump! bump! bump! the giant was home, and the hairy chap sniffed all about and said:

"Fee! Fi! Fo! Fum!
I smell the blood of an Englishman!
Be he alive, or be he dead,
I'll grind his bones to make my bread!"

"Nothing of the sort," said the big woman. "It's your tea in the tower."

But the giant said, "I smell fresh meat."

"Well," said the big woman, "if it's that youth who stole your gold and your hen, he'll be hiding himself in the oven, like as not."

But Jack wasn't in the oven; he was in the copper; so the giant didn't find him, for all he snuffled and he sniffed.

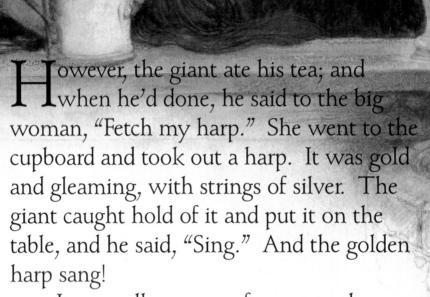

However, the giant ate his tea; and when he'd done, he said to the big woman, "Fetch my harp." She went to the cupboard and took out a harp. It was gold and gleaming, with strings of silver. The giant caught hold of it and put it on the table, and he said, "Sing." And the golden harp sang!

It sang all manner of songs to the giant: songs to make him laugh and songs to make him weep. They were songs like none Jack had ever heard before – but just then the harp began to sing a lullaby; and the giant closed his eyes and nodded off. The harp stopped its singing.

Jack crept out of the copper and went on tiptoes to the table, lifted up the harp, and started for the door. But the harp wasn't having any of that; it shouted out loud, "Master! Master!" And the giant woke up and saw Jack there by the door.

Jack didn't want any telling. He was off down the road like a shot, with the giant full tilt after him. They ran and they ran; they did run! And the harp was shouting, and the giant was roaring, and Jack was saving his breath.

He got to the top of the beanstalk and set off down; but before long he felt the beanstalk shaking. He looked up; and there was the giant on the beanstalk, climbing down after. So down went Jack; and down went the giant; and the harp was still shouting, "Master! Master!" The beanstalk wagged and bent, but it stayed stuck to the sky and didn't come loose; and at last Jack landed all of a heap in his mother's garden.

Jack's mother was lifting potatoes. "Hark!" she said. "It thunders."

"Catch hold of this harp," said Jack, "and tell it to be quiet," he said, "while I get my father's ax."

Jack gave his mother the harp; then he jumped into the house, and jumped out again with his father's ax; and he fell to chopping through the beanstalk.

The giant looked, and he saw Jack chopping, and he roared and he roared. But Jack chopped and he chopped; he chopped right through that beanstalk.

What a caterwauling! The giant swung like a plumb bob. He tried to get back up the sky; but the more he tugged, the more the sky sagged; and the more he grabbed at the beanstalk, the more it came away in his hands; until, howling and tugging, grabbing and yelling, all tangled in the beanstalk, he crashed down into the garden; and there he lay, dead as a doornail.

"That's reckoned him up," said Jack, "rump and stump, it has. Rump and stump."

And it had. But Jack and his mother,
what with the giant's gold, his red
hen, and the singing harp – well: they were
in clover. And if they're still living, they'll
be there yet.